A Just Right Book

The Snowman
Storybook

Look for The Snowman® toys, by **KIDS** Preferred™ LLC.
at a fine retailer near you.

With words by Raymond Briggs

Random House New York

In the morning James woke to see snow
falling. He ran into the garden as fast as he
could, and he started to make a snowman.

He gave him a scarf and a hat, a tangerine for
a nose, and lumps of coal for his buttons and
his eyes.

What a wonderful snowman he was! James could not go to sleep because he was thinking of his snowman.

In the middle of the night he crept down to see the snowman again. And suddenly . . . the snowman *moved*!

"Come in," said James. "But you must be very quiet."

The snowman was amazed by everything
he saw.

They even went into James's mother and
father's bedroom.

And the snowman dressed up in their clothes.

Suddenly, the snowman took James by
the hand and ran out of the house, across
the snow,

and up, up into the air.
They were flying!

James and the snowman flew for miles
through the cold, moonlight air.

Then they landed gently on the snow,
home safe in the garden.

James gave the snowman a hug and said
good night.

In the morning he was woken up by bright
sunlight shining on his face.

He must see the snowman again! James ran
out of his room, down the stairs,

across the living room, past his mother
and father,

and into the garden.